The Story of

THE LITTLE RED LEAF

by **Donna Johnson**
illustrated by **Emily Johnson**

Choice Point Editions
Stockton, California

To my grandsons, Jacob, Branden, and Andrew, and all the children who have loved participating in the telling of this tale.

And to all the teachers over the last hundred years who sustained the existence of "The Story of the Little Red Leaf".

With special thanks to: Mary Robinson, Una Belle Gaedtke, Laura Brooke, Angela Knickerbocker, Colleen Hughes, Barbara Fernandes, Mary Ulring, Margaret Rosengarten, and Bonnie Cearley.

ChoicePoint Editions
7883 North Pershing Avenue
Stockton, CA 95207

Text copyright © 2006 Donna Johnson
Illustrations copyright © 2006 Emily Johnson
Jacket design by Kathleen Bauer

Printed in China

ISBN 0-9778774-0-X

Library of Congress Control Number: 2006925443

The Story of
THE LITTLE RED LEAF

Once upon a time in the fall of the year, there was a forest of beautiful trees. All of the leaves on the trees had changed colors and fallen to the ground. All but one Little Red Leaf. He was left all alone on the tree.

If you were a Little Red Leaf, left all alone on the tree, wouldn't you be lonely?

So, the Little Red Leaf asked his Mother the Tree, "Mother the Tree, can I go down and be with the other leaves?"

His Mother the Tree said,
"No, it's not time for you to go."

Just then a group of school children from the nearby school were skipping in the leaves of the forest, gathering the most beautiful ones to take back to their classroom.

One little child stopped and looked up at the Little Red Leaf and said, "Little Red Leaf, will you come down and play with us?"

The Little Red Leaf asked his Mother the Tree, "Mother the Tree, can I go down and play with the children?"

But his Mother the Tree said, "No, it's not time for you to go."

So the school children gathered their leaves and skipped back to their classrooms.

It grew colder in the forest and all the animals knew that it was soon going to be wintertime. The squirrels were scampering about gathering nuts and leaves to line their nests.

All of a sudden, a little squirrel stopped and looked up at the Little Red Leaf and said, "Little Red Leaf, will you come down and line our nests?"

So the Little Red Leaf asked his Mother the Tree, "Mother the Tree, can I go down and line the squirrels' nests?"

But his Mother the Tree said, "No, it's not time for you to go."

So the squirrels scampered quickly back with their leaves to line their nests.

It grew colder and colder in the forest. The wind started to blow. Wheeewwww. But the Little Red Leaf still stayed on the tree.

Finally it grew quiet in the forest.

So quiet that you could hear a voice from down on the ground. Why, it was the voice of the Little Blue Flower.

The Little Blue Flower looked up at the Little Red Leaf and said, "Little Red Leaf, will you come down and cover me for the winter?"

So the Little Red Leaf asked his Mother the Tree, "Mother the Tree, can I go down and cover the Little Blue Flower for the winter?"

And his Mother the Tree said,
"Yes, it's time for you to go."
Then the wind gently blew
and the Little Red Leaf whirled

and

twirled

and

fluttered

to the ground . . .

and covered

the Little Blue Flower

for the winter.

This charming and tender little story has a folk tale-like history, loved each fall by children and parents who, upon the completion of the story and its dramatization, never fail to say "aahhh!"

It was first told in Snell's Kindergarten School in the early 1900's and later adapted and embellished in its present form by the mother-daughter team, Mary Robinson and Donna Johnson.

This first edition celebrates the 100th anniversary of Snell's Pre-Kindergarten School, in Stockton, California. Snell's Pre-Kindergarten School is one of the oldest pre-schools in the country.

Instructions for story dramatization with CD

Each child's imagination sets the stage for this dramatization. The second track of the accompanying CD offers the background music with appropriate pauses allowing the children to say their parts in the story. No props are needed, just enough room to move to the music. Children pretend to be the characters in the story; the Little Red Leaf, Mother/Father the Tree, the Skipping Children, the Scampering Squirrels, and the Little Blue Flower.

The Little Red Leaf stands tall, connected to the arm of Mother/ Father the Tree. Moving in the same direction, the Skipping Children and the Scampering Squirrels interact with the music and narration around the Little Blue Flower who sits cross-legged, pretending to be asleep near the Little Red Leaf .

When it is time for the Little Red Leaf to cover the awakening Little Blue Flower, all eyes are on the Little Red Leaf as he/she whirls and twirls to the music and narration, gently bending to cover the Little Blue Flower.